They Call Me Arty.

By Thom Uhlir,

Arty, illustrated by Grant Eaton

ISBN:1540728285
ISBN-13:9781540728289

DEDICATION

TO ANYONE THAT READS TO KIDS;
YOU ARE A HERO.

CONTENTS

ACKNOWLEDGMENTS

Thank you to my wife, Molly, who has supported me in this endeavor and helped Arty come to life. Thank you to my precious daughter who brings light to my world every day. She inspires me and provides me with new material all the time. Thank you to Rama Road Elementary, the greatest school in the USA. I really appreciate the help from Jean Childers for editing and Grant Eaton for his capturing Arty in his art work. Of course thank you to my family and friends. Some of you may see yourself in here and I can only hope it brings a smile to your face.

1. IT'S ME

Hello, my name is *Artimas Boone,* most everyone calls me *Arty.*

What a name!

My mom named me after a not so famous artist
from the
1600s. He
painted
trees. He
couldn't
have been
that good
of an
artist, no
one ever heard of him, except my mom.

Artimas, might have been cool for a name as a baby or maybe it might be cool to have that name when I'm an adult, but really, for a 3rd grader, it can be challenging to say the least.

The problem is, when the roster is called on the first day of the school year, I have to correct the teacher by saying, "That's Arty", "Not, *Artimas*", but the damage is done.

Everyone then knows my real name and so it's *"Artimas"* for a couple of weeks. I have to endure the poking fun until everyone gets tired of teasing me. My class mates then move on to the next kid. My name goes back to Arty.

The only other time I hear *"Artimas"* is when I am in trouble and my mom uses it. Then I am worried. If she says just *"Artimas,"* it's usually not bad; it means that I get some extra chores but if I hear **_Artimas Boone, come here._**" That means business and that's not a good thing for me.

"**_Artimas Boone_**", coming from mom's mouth is nothing but trouble. More than likely that is the definition of alone time with <u>NO</u> electronics. I'm then stuck doing laundry or cleaning up my room.

I guess, compared to some of the other kids it's really not too horrible.

I've heard some kids that get into trouble have to scrub the toilets for 2 weeks or do the dishes as well as weed picking in the yard.

I have even heard that there is one kid that his dad has a rock pile behind the garage and he has to move it when he gets into trouble, "One Rock at a Time."

I have never met that kid but rumor on the playground is that his arms are as big as a telephone poles. He will probably play football in high school if he survives moving the rock pile each time he misbehaves.

2. THE CHALLENGE

In class today, they announced they are having a fun run to raise money for books.

First off, why would I want to do that?

Let me get this straight. I would raise money, then run, then collect the money which means I do all that work so the school can get more books, which means I have to read more, which is more work for me.

I'm not sure, but maybe, that rock pile isn't sounding so bad.

Well, actually, I like reading....**MY STUFF!**, like "I survived shark attacks" or "How to

build your own rocket to reach the moon",
or even "How to make green blobs that
stink out of kitchen stuff", but I'm afraid
they might buy some poetry books.

*Not really **what** I like.*

The other funny part is I do like to run. I run
to my friend's house, and I run home; I run
to get my bike or run to the play ground,
but, I haven't quite figured out what a fun
run is. I also do not understand people
giving me money to run laps.

Hey, the teacher is smarter than me so she
knows something that I don't.

As she is giving instructions for the fun run,
it became obvious that there are **RULES**.
Heck, I thought running to get to one place
or the other was the only rule, but she said,
we had to do 10 laps.

Ok, I got that

"Raise money for each lap."

Ok, I think grandma is good for a couple of bucks.

"No pushing or shoving."

Ok, though you never know what happens during a competition

"and last but not least, have fun, IT'S NOT A RACE!"

I got that.......wait....did she say it's not a race? I'm sure she misspoke

I raised my hand, **"Yes Arty"**

"You did say that there is a medal for first place, Right?"

"No, if you where _listening_, this is a fun run, which means we do it for fun."

I thought to myself, doesn't the fact that we aren't racing take the fun out of it. How am I going to get 10 laps done if I can't race someone?

It may be a fun run for everyone else, but **"I"** decided, it's a race for me.

3 THE PLANNING

After school I ran home as fast as I could. I am sure I was running at least 45 miles an hour. Good thing there wasn't a police officer out there looking to ticket speeders. I am sure I would have gotten one.

I threw open the door, still running and grabbed the phone and called Grandma.

I was out of breath, when my grandma answers the phone....

"Grandma".....(pant...pant....pant)

"Yes Artimas?" (I forgot, she calls me *Artimas*, all the time.) *"Are you okay? Are you sick?"*

"No"......(pant....pant....pant) "I was running."

"You should slow down or you will kill yourself."

"It's okay grandma"......(pant.... pant...... pant) "We are having a fun run and was wondering if you could give me some money."

"Well if it's fun to run, why do you need money." She responded.

"No, no that's not what I meant. Our school is trying to raise money for books and they are having a race."

"A race? You are going to be in a race? Well then sure I can spare .50."

".50?........... I was hoping to raise a little more than that, like maybe $5.00."

"Ok Artimas, I will send you $5.00, and I hope you win. Send me a picture of your trophy."

I hung up the phone, then called my other grandparents. Sure enough, they said they would send me money and hoped I win the race.

I didn't think I would get any money. Now, I've collected a few dollars; it's time to plot a strategy on winning "**the race**."

4 THE STRATEGY

I grabbed my planning book to jot down my strategy notes. This book contained all of my serious projects and plans. Mrs. Marsh got me started using this book and I have found it to be very useful when developing a complicated strategy like this race.

I start writing; I know Stephanie is faster than me in tag, but only at the beginning of recess games. She wears out fast so I think I need to stay close to her until she tires and then **BLAST** by her.

Oh and then there's John, he seems to do well towards the end of our games but I am faster than him, so, maybe I'll put enough distance between us in the beginning and then he won't be able to catch me.

Let's see…..mmmmm……Sandy is fast, Mike, oh yeah, he is too…wow, this may be harder to win than I thought. I made my list of kids that seemed to be fast on the play ground and figured out what I would have to do to beat them.

The teacher was right, this is fun..

"To get ready to race".

5. THE RACE

After days of planning and plotting my strategy;

It was race day.....at least for me.....Fun run for everyone else. I have it all figured out.

The sun was out, nice and bright on this spring day. I noticed everything, the birds chirping, the beautiful trees, the light breeze on my face, even the smell of the grass that was freshly cut. My mind was sharp and ready to race.

Our class went out to the race area and I looked around and paused in shock.

WHAT? ....the whole school is out there, ***all the kids***.

Not only that, I found out that we aren't running with just my class but the whole grade...I didn't plot that strategy out.

I know some of those kids and they are fast....I mean real fast but I am sure they didn't plot out a race like I did and I am sure they think it's a fun run.

I kept telling myself as we walked to the starting line, Ok, Arty, don't panic, stick to the plan.

"Ok, everyone, this is a fun run." Mrs. Marsh,
announce in her megaphone.

"There are a couple of rules.....Remember THIS IS A FUN RUN..........................NOT A RACE....."

That's what she thinks, I thought.

"Also, no pushing or shoving, be nice to your classmates and friends."...............

"Oh, yes, and remember to pace yourself......"

I was looking around; some of these kids look serious. Come on Arty just relax, I kept repeating to myself, just run with the faster kids and then the last 2 laps, **ZOOM Away**, just the way I planned it.

Mrs. Marsh, Announced

"Ready......
Set......GOOOOOOOOOOO!"

Everyone took off, some of the kids sprinted ahead but I knew better and I hung back a little, and it's a good thing.

Around the first corner, Andy from the

other class cut off a couple of kids and then fell, knocking 3 kids to the grass. It was like an accident on the highway.

Mrs. Marsh ran over and gave him a talking to while all the other kids ran by looking at their classmates on the ground.

A couple of other kids ran into each other and they fell. That is what they get for looking at the turmoil and not looking to see where they were going. They where colliding like bowling pins.

I made it past the corner and was thinking 4 kids hurt and Andy getting an ear full before running again, at this rate I will be the only one running by lap 8.

Victory is MINE!!!!!!

The first lap went pretty fast as the next
several did too. As the excitement of the
start wore off I looked around. There was
Stephanie way ahead, just like I thought,
she took off too fast....at least I hope
so....Sandy and Mike, there they are.

That kid from Mrs. Flower's room, is
running with them. I'm just behind that
group, with John, who is right behind me.

Everything seems to be working as planned.

I'm starting to breathe a little bit more and
my legs are getting a little tired. They feel a
little heavy as we did another lap.

I finally passed Stephanie, she was
breathing real hard and stopped to walk.
Great! My game plan is working,

I'm brilliant!

I can hear the rest of the school cheering everyone on. They think it's a race too. With all the kids standing around and yelling it feels like I am running in a stadium, with fans cheering me on.

That's right; I'm at the Olympics with thousands of people cheering me on. I'm starting to get a little tired but with all those people in the stadium yelling, I don't want to let them down or let my country down. I push on with each turn and **"each lap"**.

There is lap 5, half way there. Uhhhhhhhh,
I'm getting a little more fatigued. These
laps are taking longer. Did someone
lengthen the laps?............ No, they didn't,
but it sure feels like each lap has become
longer and the track seems bigger.

There is Mike and Sandy, they are still
running together but I'm catching them.

My legs are getting a little more tired but
I'm doing ok. I put my head down and
push past Mike and then
Sandy.....yes....with 3 laps left,
I have taken the lead.....oh yes,

Victory!

The crowd gets louder in the Olympic
Stadium as they are cheering the runners
on.....specifically **Me**.....I can get a gold
medal as long as I can last these
last few laps.

My lungs are breathing deep and hard, my legs are really tire, and I'm thirsty, but Olympic runners don't drink water in the middle of a race. I will just have to wait.

I look over my shoulder and **WHAT?**.....John! .....He is still there.....What is he doing there?......There isn't suppose to be anyone there. That wasn't part of my plan. I was sure he would have dropped back by now.

I think he has the same game plan as me. By the look on his face, he thinks this a race.

 I should tell him it's a fun run.

    I'm breathing hard and between breaths,
"John"....pant...pant....pant *"you know this is just a fun"*....pant...pant....pant *"run and not a race"*.....pant.... pant... pant

"*I know*", he responded. At least I could tell he was breathing hard too.......and then picked up the pace and passed me.

Well, that didn't work. Ok, now it's him against me.

I move right behind him.

We are now in an all out race for the Olympic Gold Medal. The crowd is going wild. The noise is so loud I can't hear myself breathing.

My lungs start to burn, trying to get more oxygen. My legs are heavy, I look down to see if I am running in mud....no...there's no mud, just my tired legs.

2 laps to go......wow....I'm really tired but John is right in front of me and I'm not going to let him beat me.

The crowd is screaming now....then it

started, only with a few and now its louder and louder as I run around the curve………

ARTY……ARTY…..ARTY…..

They are chanting my name….I can't let them down now…..they are my fans……

ARTY….ARTY…..ARTY……

Go Arty Go

I start using my arms more and more.

John is good….I can barely keep up…..one lap left…..

ARTY….ARTY….ARTY…..

If I can win my fans will carry me out

of the stadium on their shoulders.

I am barely hanging on, my legs are so tired and my breathing is hard and fast. Even my head is moving back and forth.

One lap left…..John against Me….Gold Medal for the winner!…..around the turn, pumping my arms, and then it happens…..

John seemed to slow a half a step….I keep using my arm….pumping them around the 2nd turn, half a lap to go……

I move around John, he is pumping his arms; we are running next to each other…. I got another half step….The Olympic stadium roars as my fans chant my name…..

ARTY….ARTY….ARTY…

there is the 3rd turn….one turn left…..I am a half step ahead, I can feel him right behind me….the forth turn….I'm pumping my arms, using my legs as best as I can…..

I lunge for the finish line…..I break the yellow champion tape and stumble to the ground…..

YESSSSS, I won…..I am bringing the gold medal home…….

I am laying there breathing hard, legs are burning, my yellow t-shirt is bunched up around me, making it look like the finishing championship tape.

I'm waiting for my fans to pick me up and carry me to the victory stand; then out of the stadium on their shoulders…..I feel someone pick me up….yes, my fans….

6. THE WINNER

"Get up Artimas", Mrs. Marsh bellowed....***"What do you think this is, some kind of race or something....get some water and don't be so dramatic next time."***

I am sure Mrs. Marsh is from some country that didn't have a runner in the race today or else she would have been nicer to the "Gold Medal Winner".

I get my water, and look around, no one is looking at me, no one is coming to pick me up, no one is carrying me out of the stadium....... I guess they don't know what to say to the winner, that is ok, it's tough being an Olympic Champion.

Everyone walks over to where the award ceremony is. I just can't wait to get my first place prize.

Mrs. Marsh is talking about how fun it was and for once I agreed with her, it was fun....to win......and then the moment is there*......"**And the winner**"* She announces *is....Audrey Helms."*

WHO? ....I am sure she got confused and just missed my name......

She continued, ***"Yes, Audrey raised the most money and is the winner of the Fun Run.... thank you everyone for participating."***

Everyone went over to Audrey and practically carried her back to the school on their shoulders.

I stood there, stunned, not sure what just happened. I had my head hung low as I

tried to figure out what went wrong. I slowly followed the crowd back to the school.

John and Mike came up to me and shook my hand and said **"Good race."**

I looked at them and was surprised that they were so nice to me after I beat both of them. **"Arty, it was fun racing, and you were really fast."**

"Yes it was fun racing and you are very fast too." I responded.

Mrs. Marsh came up and said, ***"Good race boys."*** She said with a grin.

We were the last ones entering the school.

She said. ***"I knew what you kids were doing, even though it was supposed to be a fun run, I know you were racing."***

She continued, **"Audrey is the one that won. Sometimes the prize doesn't always go to first place. Remember; it's the journey and how you got there** *that is important. Audrey probably learned more than you did today."*

"Competition brings out the best and worst in people. Make sure when you are competing it brings out the best in you by being a humbled winner and gracious loser. Above all, don't forget about your friends. They will rejoice with you and help you when you're down."

"Now get inside and congratulate Audrey."

We walked inside and looked at how happy Audrey was and it made me happy too. Even though I didn't get a medal, I started to realize there are different ways to win.

What a great day for a fun run!

Years later........I was thinking about that day of the fun run. The air seemed so perfect; the sun so bright, just like it is today. I remember Mrs. Marsh and those words she said after the fun run. I remember all the lessons I learned that year in third grade and I was grateful. I was happy to still have my best friends, John and Mike. They are here, sitting close by, but I don't know exactly where. All those lessons and friendships I brought with me today, as I stepped out onto the track, in front of 70,000 people at the Olympics.

ABOUT THE AUTHOR

Thom Uhlir grew up in Champaign, Illinois and now lives in Charlotte, NC. He received his Bachelors degree from Eastern Illinois University in Education and received his Masters Degree from University of North Carolina at Charlotte. He has spent the last 30 years as a fitness trainer. In his spare time, Thom likes to run, bike, hike, play tennis, read and write short stories.

.

Made in the USA
Columbia, SC
25 May 2021